TALL
TALES

SIX AMAZING BASKETBALL DREAMS

TEXT + IMAGES BY

CHARLES R. SMITH JR.

DUTTON CHILDREN'S BOOKS • NEW YORK

ACKNOWLEDGMENTS + THANK-YOUS

THE MAKING OF THIS BOOK REQUIRED A VERY LARGE EFFORT FROM MANY PEOPLE, TO WHOM I AM VERY GRATEFUL.

ALL OF MY GREAT "ACTORS": CARLI ("SABINE"), NICOLE, AND LISA IANNOTTO AND IVANA PALMA ("JO"), KEEP DOING YOUR THING ON THE COURTS AND IN SCHOOL. EDSON, I HOPE YOU HAD A GOOD TIME IN THE U.S. OVER THE SUMMER. LANNI MILES, THANKS FOR DOING THIS ON SHORT NOTICE; KEEP BREAKING 'EM DOWN. O'SHANE WALKER, DO YOUR SOCCER THING IN SYRACUSE AND CONGRATULATIONS ON THE SCHOLARSHIP. JERMAL ("THE MAIN EVENT"), WHAT CAN I SAY—YOU, KIRK, GARY, AND RAHSHEEM STARTED IT ALL. THANKS FOR SETTING THE STANDARD.

TO ALL INVOLVED, I HOPE YOU HAD AS GOOD A TIME BEING PHOTOGRAPHED AS I DID PHOTOGRAPHING YOU.

 ● Library of Congress Cataloging-in-Publication Data ● Smith, Charles R., Jr. ● Tall Tales/ by Charles R. Smith Jr.—1st ed. ● p. cm. ● Summary: In this collection of stories illustrated with photographs, youngsters show off their smooth moves on the basketball court. ● ISBN 0-525-46172-8 (hc) ● 1. Children's stories, American. 2. Basketball stories. ● [1. Basketball—Fiction. 2. Short stories.] I. Title. ● PZ7.S6438Tal 2000 [Fic]—dc21 99-31567 CIP AC ● Published in the United States by Dutton Children's Books, a division of Penguin Putnam Books for Young Readers, 345 Hudson Street, New York, New York 10014 ● http://www.penguinputnam.com/yreaders/index.htm ● Designed by Ellen M. Lucaire ● Printed in Hong Kong ● First Edition ● 1 2 3 4 5 6 7 8 9 10

This book is dedicated to my nieces and nephews, who make up my family's next generation: Skyler, T.J. and Alex, Jessica and Hannah, and Katie. And to our own new entry into the family, Sabine. Your energy and love motivate me to write books for you and future generations.

CONTENTS

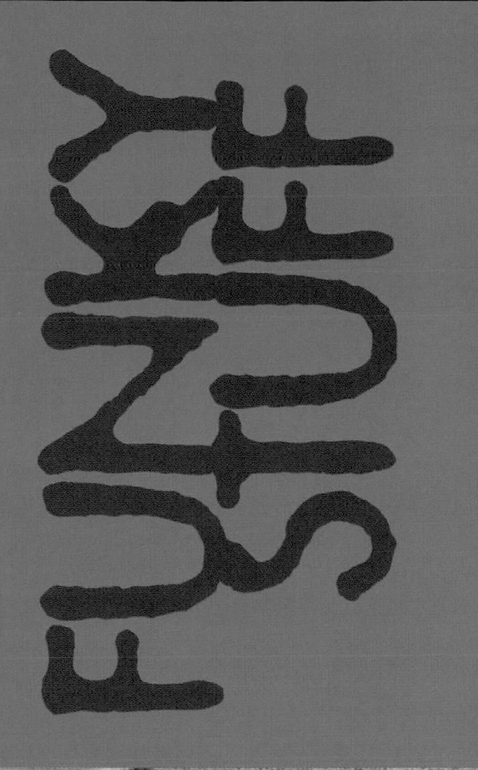

What Jo Did

Little Joanna Marie loved to play basketball. She especially loved the sound the ball made as it fell through the net. She would practice every day, touching the backboard as often as she could. Since Joanna's parents had no idea how high a basketball rim should be, they hung it on the side of their roof, which was a whopping sixteen feet high. • Joanna saw rims on TV and figured they looked about the same height as her own—she had no idea they were only ten feet high. • Joanna also didn't realize that most people couldn't jump up and touch the backboard because she hadn't ever played with anyone else. But her parents marveled at how high she jumped, and how she could run up to the backboard with the ball and lay it up and in. Her father was especially proud because he couldn't even touch the bottom of the net. Not even with the help of a broom.

One day Joanna, her hair bundled up under her baseball cap, was dribbling her basketball on the way to the store to get some sugar for her mother. Her mother said that she didn't have to hurry home, as long as she was in by dark. As Joanna moved down the street, a basketball came rolling out of nowhere and bumped her high-tops. • "I'm sorry, man, I didn't mean to hit you with the ball like that," said a young boy dressed in sneakers, shorts, and a Bulls tank top as he picked up the ball. • "Oh, that's okay. I wasn't even paying attention," Joanna said. • "Hey, we need one more to play a game. You in?" he asked her. • "Sure, why not?" she responded. • As Joanna approached the other boys, she remembered that she had her hat on. • They probably think I'm a boy, she thought. Might as well enjoy the ride.

The boys picked teams, and since Joanna was smaller than everyone else, she got picked last. It didn't bother her, though, because she had never played with anyone before and was just happy to be there. • "Hey, kid, what's your name?" asked a freckle-faced kid with red hair. • "Ahhh . . . Jo. My name is Jo," Joanna said nervously. • "All right, Joe, you pick up T.J. over there, see. Make sure he doesn't score a basket. He can jump pretty high, ya know!" • Jo moved around, not really touching the ball at first, just trying to get a feel for playing with other people. She had never even passed the ball or received a pass herself. Playing with others took getting used to, but in no time she was passing the ball. The only thing that puzzled her was why the hoop was so low. • Even though the boys passed the ball around a lot, T.J. didn't really touch it much, and when he did, he didn't take a shot. Finally, he was wide open for a jump shot when Jo came out of nowhere, jumped high into the air, and swatted his shot into the next court. • "Wow, did you see that? Did you see how high he jumped?" the freckle-faced kid said, his mouth wide open. • "I've never seen anybody jump that high. Not even Michael Jordan," said the kid with the Bulls jersey on.

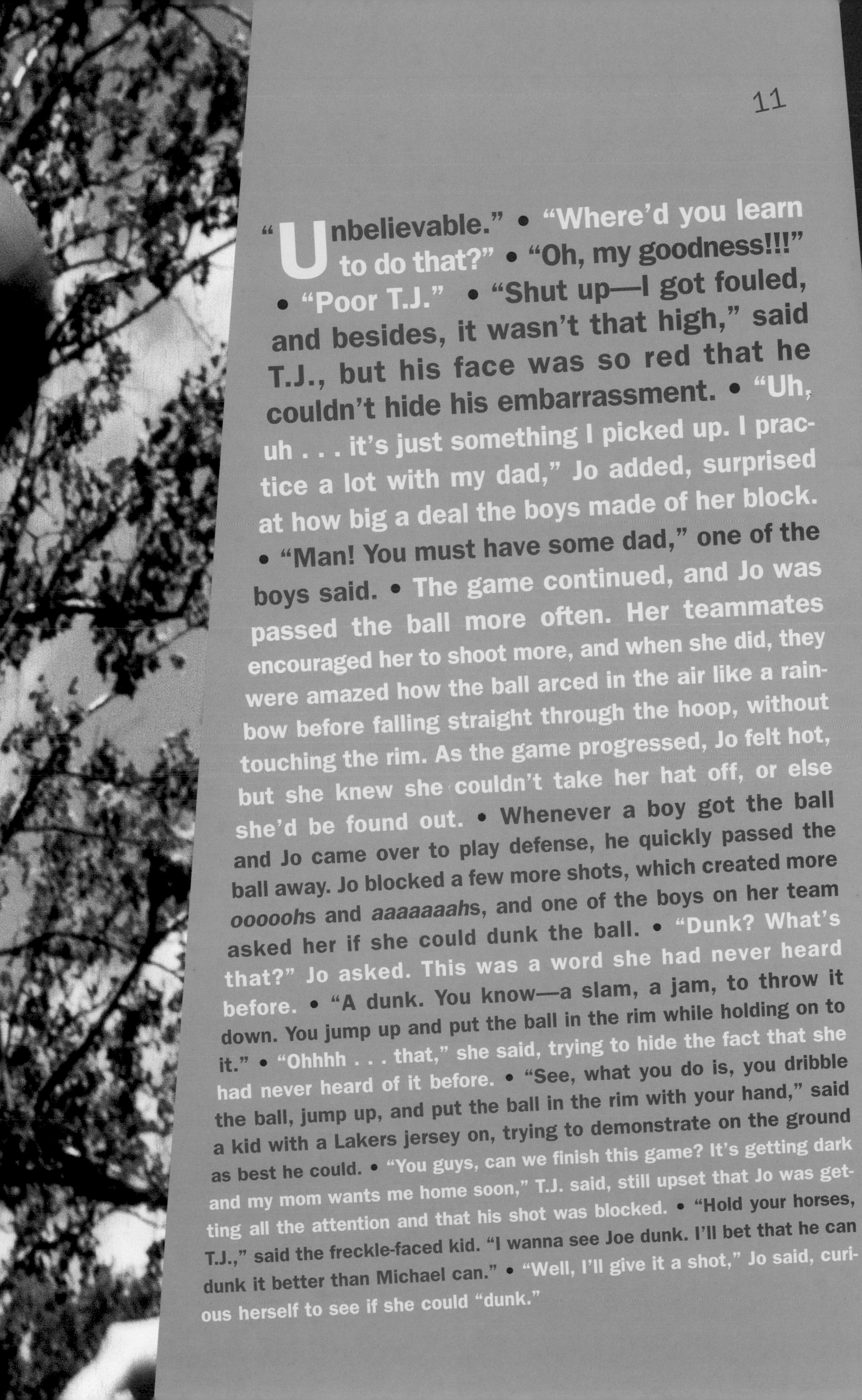

"Unbelievable." • "Where'd you learn to do that?" • "Oh, my goodness!!!" • "Poor T.J." • "Shut up—I got fouled, and besides, it wasn't that high," said T.J., but his face was so red that he couldn't hide his embarrassment. • "Uh, uh . . . it's just something I picked up. I practice a lot with my dad," Jo added, surprised at how big a deal the boys made of her block. • "Man! You must have some dad," one of the boys said. • The game continued, and Jo was passed the ball more often. Her teammates encouraged her to shoot more, and when she did, they were amazed how the ball arced in the air like a rainbow before falling straight through the hoop, without touching the rim. As the game progressed, Jo felt hot, but she knew she couldn't take her hat off, or else she'd be found out. • Whenever a boy got the ball and Jo came over to play defense, he quickly passed the ball away. Jo blocked a few more shots, which created more *oooooh*s and *aaaaaaah*s, and one of the boys on her team asked her if she could dunk the ball. • "Dunk? What's that?" Jo asked. This was a word she had never heard before. • "A dunk. You know—a slam, a jam, to throw it down. You jump up and put the ball in the rim while holding on to it." • "Ohhhh . . . that," she said, trying to hide the fact that she had never heard of it before. • "See, what you do is, you dribble the ball, jump up, and put the ball in the rim with your hand," said a kid with a Lakers jersey on, trying to demonstrate on the ground as best he could. • "You guys, can we finish this game? It's getting dark and my mom wants me home soon," T.J. said, still upset that Jo was getting all the attention and that his shot was blocked. • "Hold your horses, T.J.," said the freckle-faced kid. "I wanna see Joe dunk. I'll bet that he can dunk it better than Michael can." • "Well, I'll give it a shot," Jo said, curious herself to see if she could "dunk."

She
started at
half-court,
dribbling
the ball quickly,
and headed
straight for the rim.
As she approached,
she remembered
how high her basket
was and realized that this
one was much lower.
Maybe she *could*
jump a little farther out
and dunk the ball through.
As she got to the free throw line,
she lifted her left leg up
and went flying into the air,
till she was so high she was
looking down on the hoop.
Now all she had to do was
put the ball in the rim with both hands.

She was up there for a while
before she felt her hands on the rim,
the ball going through,
and her feet touching the ground.

When she landed,

all of the boys' mouths were hanging open,

and for a moment they were speechless.

Then:

"No way."

"It can't be!"

"Am I seeing right?"

"That's impossible."

"How did she . . . ?"

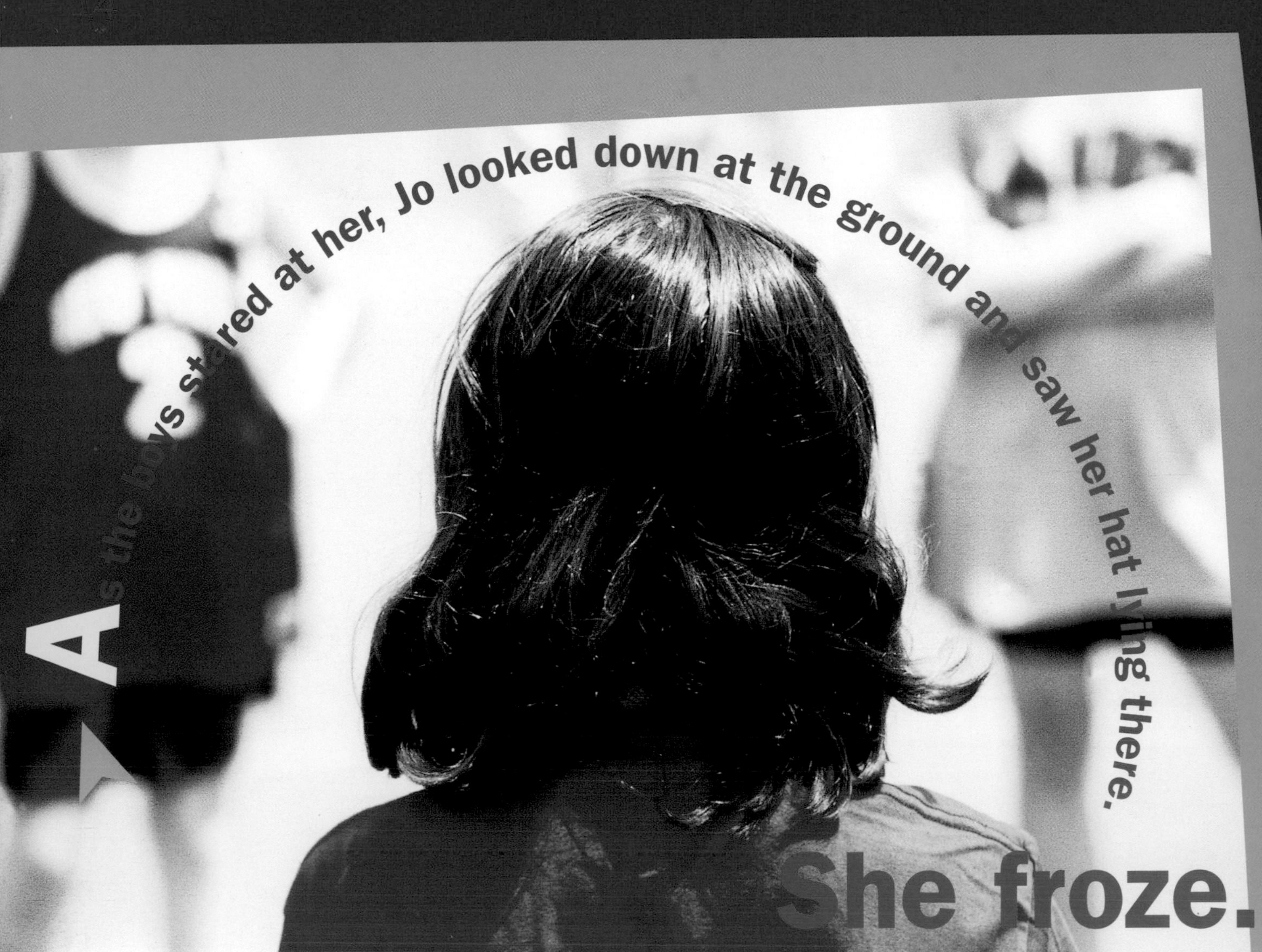

As the boys stared at her, Jo looked down at the ground and saw her hat lying there.

She froze.

"So, like . . . you're a girl?" said the kid with the Lakers jersey.

"Ahhhh . . . yeah . . . you could say that," Jo answered slowly.

"Omigod. I can't believe it, you guys, we've been playing basketball with a girl," T.J. said with disgust.

"Hey, she may be a girl, but I'd play on her team anytime." The kid with the Bulls jersey approached Jo and gave her a high five.

After that, they congratulated Jo and introduced themselves. They even came up with a nickname for her: Jumpin' Jo. In the end, T.J. walked up to her and apologized.

"Sorry, Jo," he whispered. "I just never played against a girl before. Especially a girl as good as you. I've never seen anyone who can jump like that! You should come and play with us again sometime. But next time, leave the hat at home."

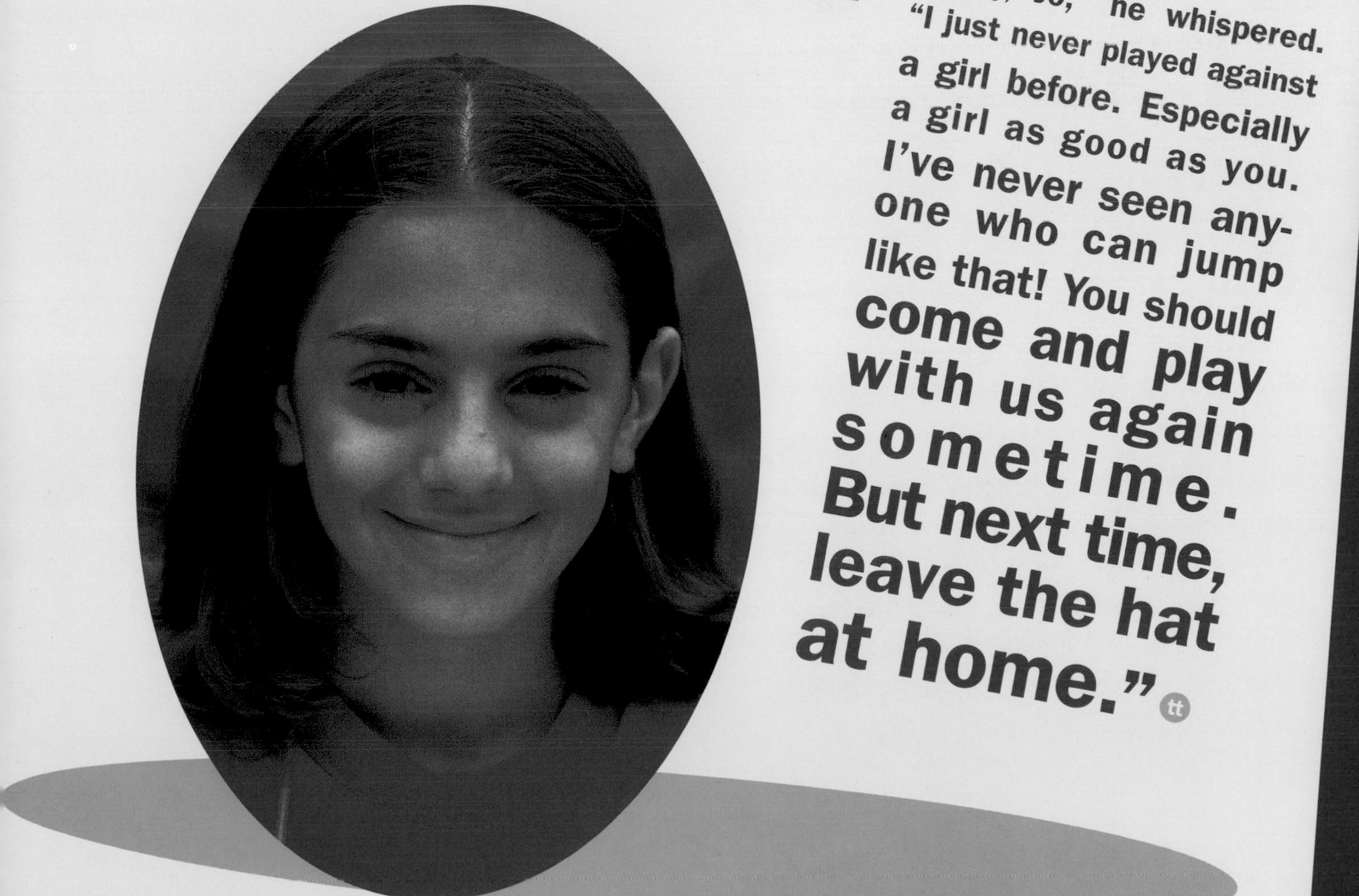

WALK SOFTLY

Big John was the quiet type. Never really said much. Didn't really need to. Just walked softly and carried a big jump shot. When he showed up at the park to play, everyone would whisper. His jump shot was like that.

But that wasn't the only reason people whispered. See, John didn't speak much, and since he was very quiet, lies and rumors spread about him:

John didn't talk much because he was dropped on his head as a child. John didn't talk much because the ghost of his grandfather had scared his voice out of him. John didn't talk much

because his mother used to keep their cat in the same room when he was a baby, and the cat got his tongue. John didn't talk much because . . .

Rumors spread faster than wildfire, but John didn't let the flames burn him. Usually, those who are silent speak in other ways.

His silence wasn't the only thing that people noticed about John. They also noticed that he wore dark sunglasses when he played. But nobody paid as much attention to the glasses as they did to his silence, because he *was* playing in the bright sun. That is, nobody noticed until one day when someone knocked off his glasses trying to block his shot. They fell to the ground, and as play continued, he knelt on the ground and fumbled around for them. He fumbled around for them as if he couldn't see them. It turns out that he couldn't. He was blind. Imagine that. Blind!

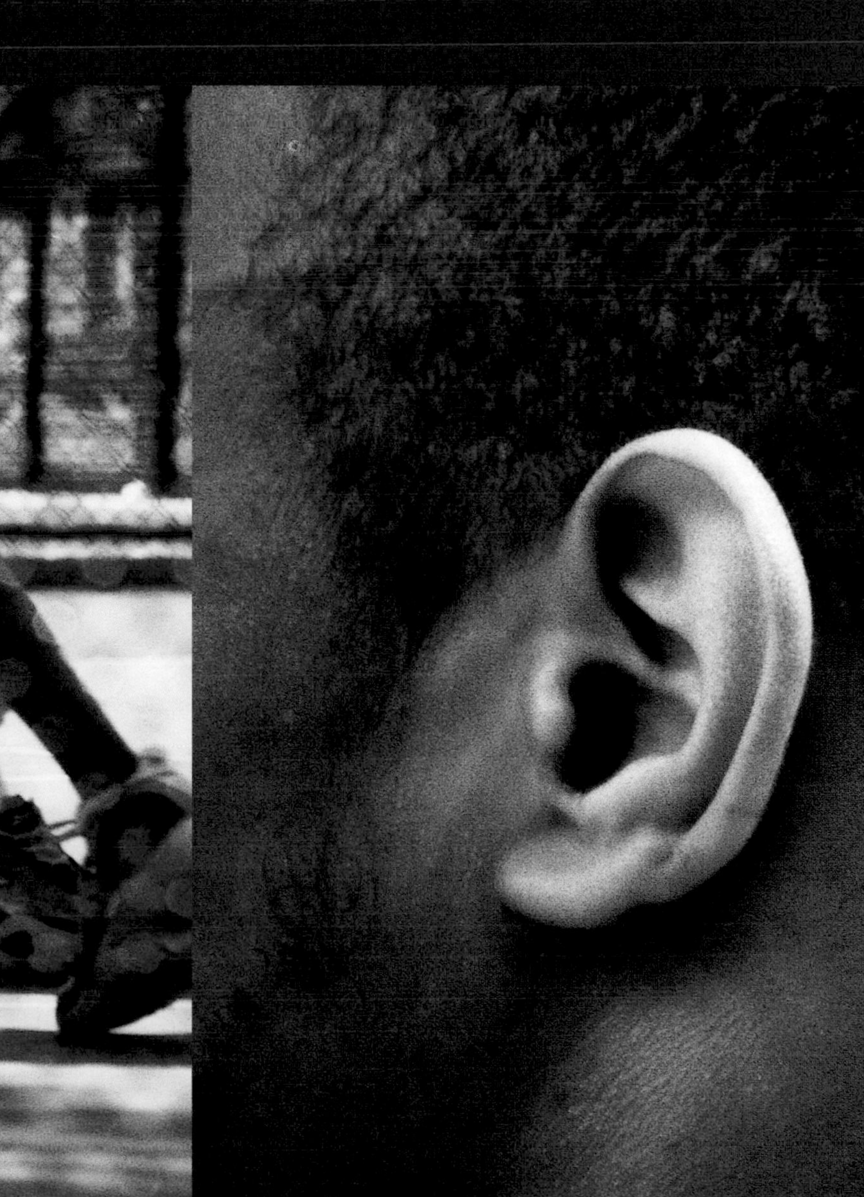

Play on the court stopped immediately when everyone began to realize that the guy with the best jump shot in the park couldn't even see it go through the net. The guy who had fouled John picked the glasses up, handed them to him, told him he had fouled him, and said it was John's ball.

After the game was over, a brave soul approached John and quietly asked him why he hadn't told anyone.

"Why should I? Do you think anyone would believe that a blind man can play ball?" John answered, smiling.

The young man agreed and then asked John why he didn't talk much. "Are you deaf?"

“No, I’m not deaf. But since I can’t see what I’m doing, I like to keep quiet so I can at least hear what I’m doing. I love to hear the rhythmic bounce of the ball. The sound a pass makes when someone catches it right in their hands. The shuffling of feet on concrete. And most of all, the ball going through the net.”

The young man nodded in agreement as John continued, “The sound of the ball being caressed by the nylon cords is so beautiful that it speaks louder than I ever could, and I don’t want to interrupt it.”

MUST BE THE SHOES

S

Great how am I supposed to do that I can t just make myself grow I m never gonna get to play with you

Sabine hated seeing her brothers play games like H-O-R-S-E, 21, or one-on-one, knowing that she couldn't join in.

"Grow? I don't need to grow, I just need to be good!" She got up from her chair in the backyard and headed for her room. Once there, she flopped on her bed and stared at the ceiling.

"There's got to be something I can do. I could practice . . . but every park I've gone to, the boys don't want to play with me. Well, I'll show them!" she said, her mind ticking away.

As she lay there thinking, she dozed off. Suddenly she heard a loud crash. It sounded as if it came from her closet. She jumped off her bed and ran to see what the noise was. As she walked toward it, the closet door opened. All her clothes and shoes were gone; the only thing inside was a pair of **glowing white sneakers**.

"Hey, what happened to all my clothes? And whose sneakers are these?"

She looked around the room to see if one of her brothers was playing a trick on her. Then the shoes moved. They rumbled, they shook, and before she knew it, they jumped on Sabine's feet.

"What's going on here?" she whispered, peeking over her shoulder.

"Ha-ha. Very funny, you guys! I'm gonna tell Mom that you took my clothes," she said as she walked over to her window. But down below, she saw her brothers still on the court.

She stared at
the glowing shoes, suddenly feeling an urge to play basketball with her brothers, whether they let her or not. As she stepped outside, her feet tingled, and her arms felt very strong. She was on a mission. She stepped outside just as the ball rolled onto the grass.

"Hey, Sabine, could you throw it back?" her brother Adrian asked.

"No, you know what—why don't you shoot the ball, Sabine?" said her other brother, Andrew.

"Yeah, Sabine, shoot the ball," Adrian said, laughing. "You can do it. You're only—what—thirty feet away! You can make that, no problem."

Adrian and Andrew kept teasing her. Their voices became more irritating by the minute.

"Grow up!" they said. "Get taller!" they said. "Learn how to play! You can't shoot the ball from thirty feet away!"

Oh yeah?

Well, I'll show them, Sabine thought.
"Watch this," she said.

She grabbed the ball, brought it behind her head, and aimed in one quick motion. Then her arms went forward, and she released the ball in a single smooth stroke. It sailed through the air with a sweet spin on it and went cleanly through the net with a

SWISH!

"Huh! Beginner's luck. I'll bet you can't do that again," Andrew said.

Without a word, Sabine grabbed the ball and proceeded to put on a show. She dribbled behind her back, between her legs, and around her brothers.

Her shoes led the way, and she went along. She made shots from under the basket, shots from the side of the basket, close up, and far away. She even made a shot from behind the basket! Her brothers watched with their mouths open. Their sister was doing things that they could only dream of, and for her grand finale, she went thirty-five feet away from the basket, turned around, threw the ball over her head . . .

and hit nothing but net.

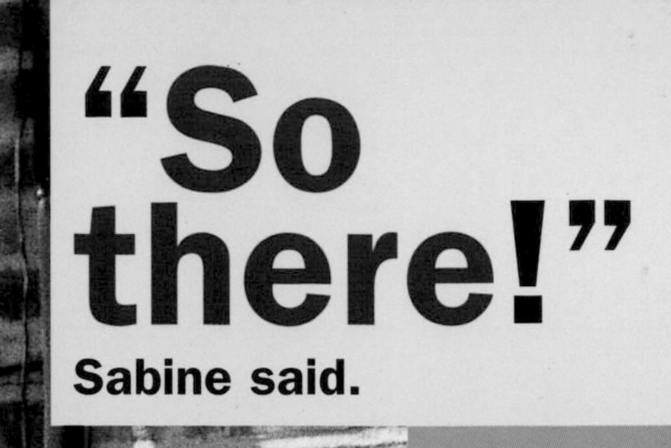

"So there!"

Sabine said.

"Ahhh . . . you know what, Sabine? I think you grew a couple of inches,"

Andrew said.

"A couple? More like a bunch. Maybe it's those shoes. Are those new shoes you're wearing, Sabine?"

Adrian asked, pointing at her sneakers.

"They're awfully bright."

"These old things? Nah, I just found them buried in my closet."

"Are you sure? I've never seen them before. I wonder if that's why you played so well."

"No way! Shoes can't do that," Andrew said, staring at the glowing sneakers.

"Anyway, I think you're ready to play with us now," said Adrian. He stared at the rim and then at his sister again.

"Wrong. I think you guys are finally ready to play with me," she said, grabbing the ball and dribbling circles around her brothers.

FUNKY

"WHEW!!! That shirt STINKS," the young ballplayer said, taking a seat against the fence after a HOT game of three-on-three. "That shirt SMELLS so BAD it could probably WALK by ITSELF."

"MAN, I had a SHIRT that smelled SO bad my mom KEPT it in a PLASTIC BAG in the GARAGE even when it was CLEAN," added a bare-chested player bouncing a basketball.

"Oh, YOU think THAT'S bad? I had some SHORTS that smelled SO BAD they SET off FIRE ALARMS," said an older player in faded shorts and an OLD sweatshirt.

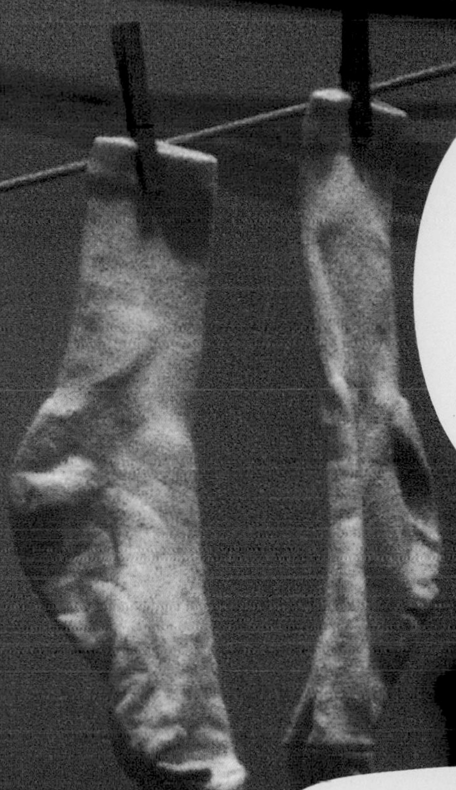

"SOUNDS LIKE YOU'RE TALKING ABOUT ROSES. I HAD SOME SOCKS THAT WERE SO NASTY, I USED THEM TO KEEP FLIES OUT OF THE HOUSE. ONE WHIFF AND THEY DROPPED DEAD," SAID ANOTHER PLAYER WEARING BROWN SHORTS AND A GREEN SHIRT.

"THAT'S PERFUME YOU'RE DESCRIBING! I HAD SOME SHOES THAT SMELLED SO BAD, WHEN I TRIED TO BURN THEM, THE FLAMES KEPT JUMPING OUT OF THE WAY!" ADDED AN OLD MAN SEATED IN WRINKLED SWEATPANTS AND A HOLEY SHIRT.

"OH, PLEASE! YOU GUYS ARE TALKING ABOUT A GARDEN! I ONCE HAD A SHIRT, SOME SHORTS, SOCKS, AND SHOES THAT WERE SO FUNKY, THEY NOT ONLY WALKED BY THEMSELVES BUT PLAYED ME ONE-ON-ONE, BEAT ME WORSE THAN I BEAT YOU, AND TALKED TRASH DOING IT!!" ADDED A PLAYER DRESSED IN A BRIGHT RED JERSEY, CLEAN BLACK-MESH SHORTS, CRISP WHITE SOCKS, AND FRESH JORDANS AS HE BOUNCED HIS BALL OUT OF THE PARK. tt

STUFF

i like to break ankles.

That's what we call it when you make your defender look so bad that he falls while trying to steal the ball. Usually I fake left, then go right, and then—**KRA-KRAK**—he looks silly. He got shook. Shook to the ground.

You know why it happens so much? Because he always goes after the ball. But he'll never get it. Not from me, he won't. That's because I dribble the ball so well that it looks like the ball is on a string.

When I get going, I can make the ball do anything I want. I can make it travel around my body, between my legs, behind my back, even off my knee. And that's with either hand, not just my right. I can make it go away and come back to me if I want. You don't believe me, do you? All right then, let me tell you what happened in this game one time.

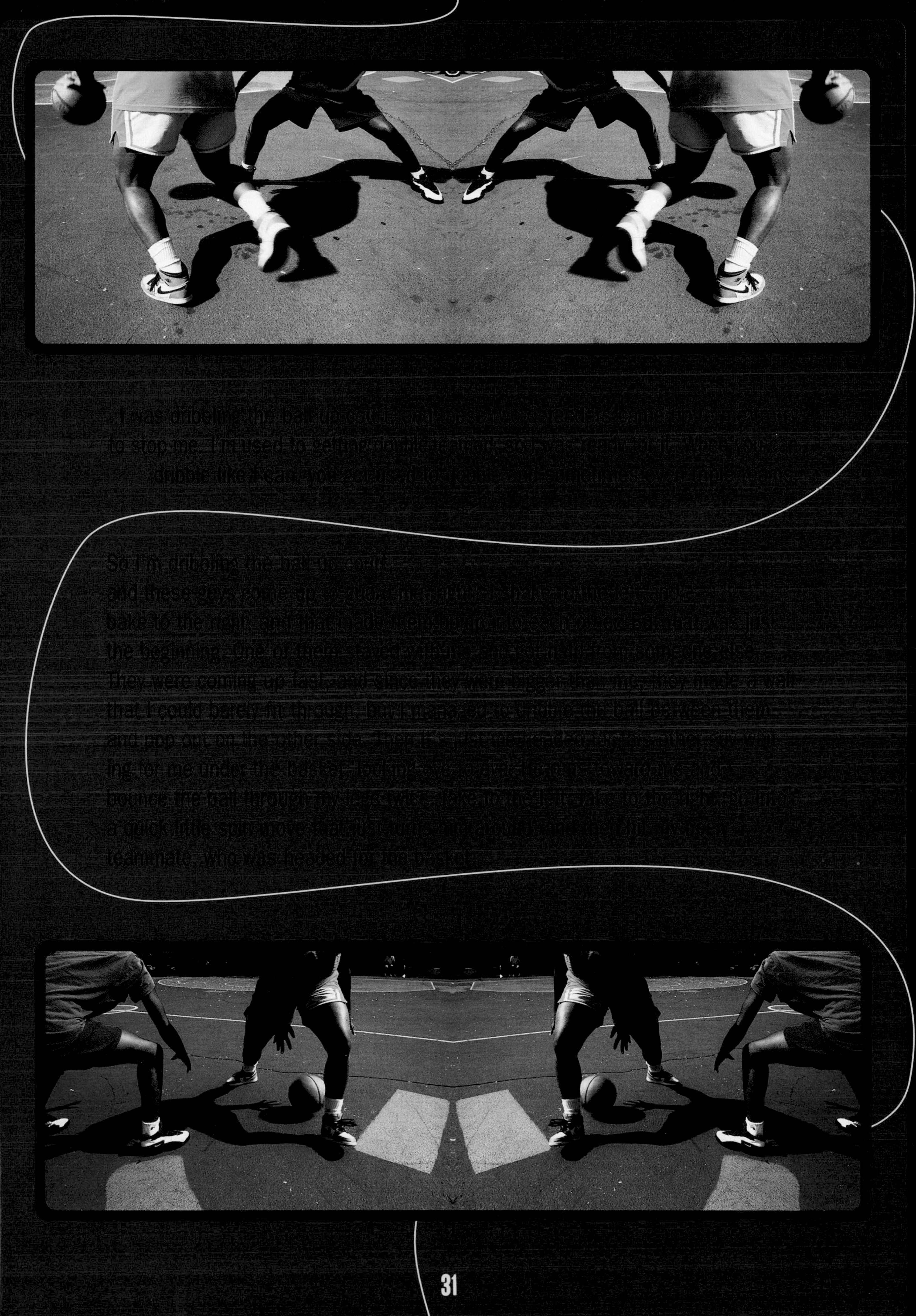

I was dribbling the ball up court, and these two defenders came up to me to try to stop me. I'm used to getting double-teamed, so I was ready for it. When you can dribble like I can, you get used to double- and sometimes even triple-teams.

So I'm dribbling the ball up court and these guys come up to guard me, right? I fake to the left and fake to the right, and that made them bump into each other. But that was just the beginning. One of them stayed with me and got help from someone else. They were coming up fast, and since they were bigger than me, they made a wall that I could barely fit through, but I managed to dribble the ball between them and pop out on the other side. Then it's just me headed for this other guy waiting for me under the basket, looking eye to eye. He runs toward me, and I bounce the ball through my legs twice, fake to the left, fake to the right, go into a quick little spin move that just turns him around, and then hit my open teammate, who was headed for the basket.

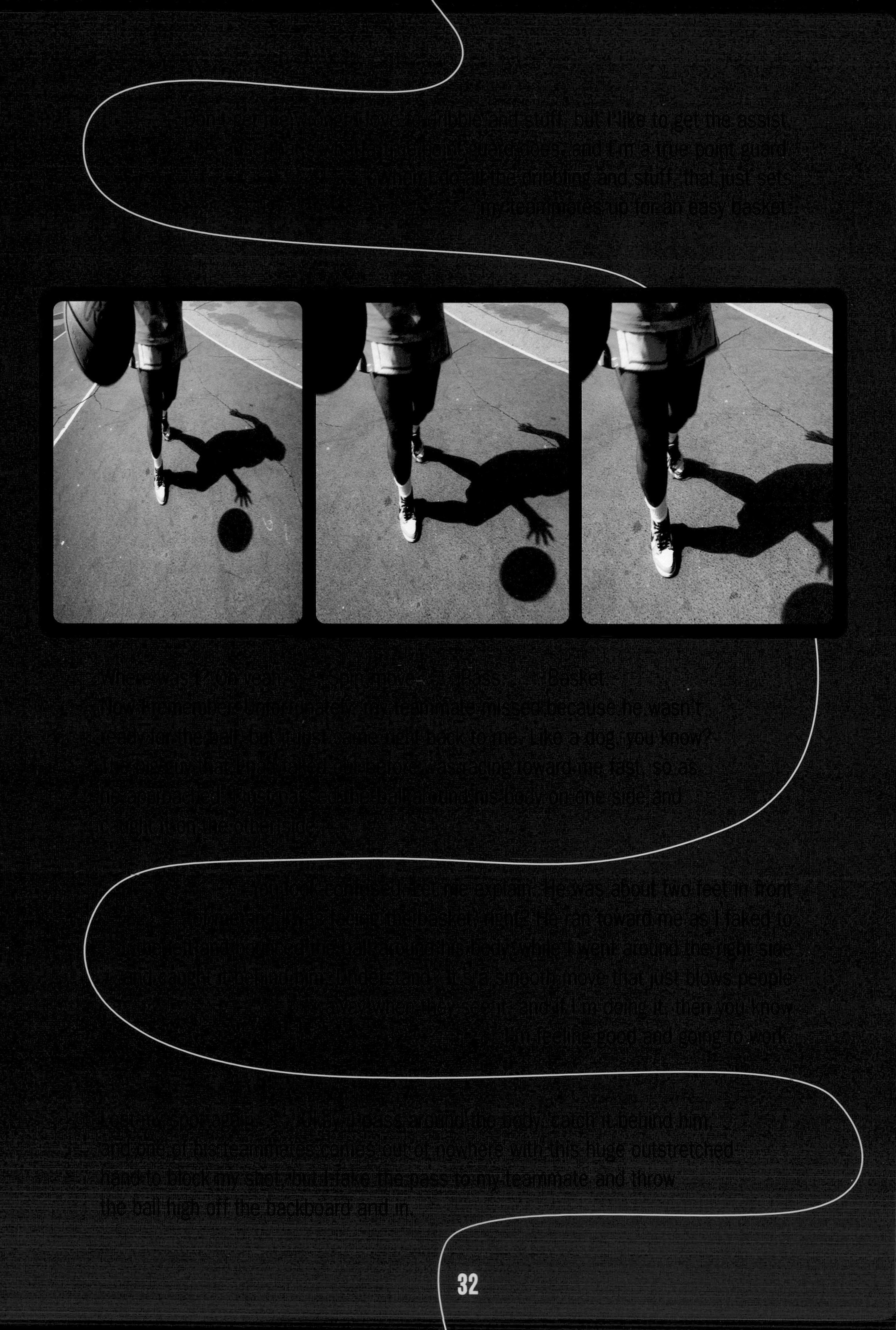

Don't get me wrong. I love to dribble and stuff, but I like to get the assist, because that's what a true point guard does, and I'm a true point guard. When I do all the dribbling and stuff, that just sets my teammates up for an easy basket.

Where was I? Oh yeah . . . Spin move → Pass → Basket.
Now I remember. Unfortunately, my teammate missed because he wasn't ready for the ball, but it just came right back to me. Like a dog, you know? The last [illegible] was heading toward me fast, so as he approached I just passed the ball around his body on one side and caught it on the other side.

You look confused. Let me explain. He was about two feet in front of me [illegible] the basket, right? He ran toward me as I faked to the left and passed the ball around his body while I went around the right side and caught it behind him. Understand? It's a smooth move that just blows people away when they see it, and if I'm doing it, then you know I'm feeling good and going to work.

I'm in my spot again [illegible] pass around the body, catch it behind him, and one of his teammates comes out of nowhere with this huge outstretched hand to block my shot, but I fake the pass to my teammate and throw the ball high off the backboard and in.

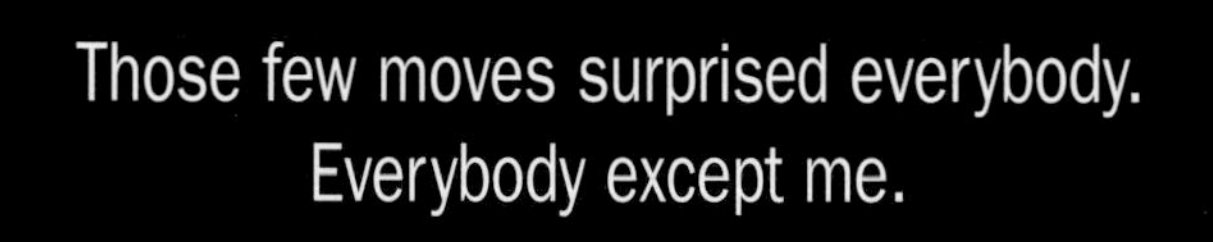

Those few moves surprised everybody.
Everybody except me.

THE MAIN EVENT

. . . I remember this one time this guy came into the park, right? Real big guy. Not just tall, but real strong. Called himself "The Main Event." The Main Event?! What kind of name is that? Sounded like a boxing match or something. I thought he called himself that because he liked to fight and beat people up. Man, was I wrong!!!

After watching him play for the first few minutes, I couldn't quite figure him out. He was good, and sure he could play, but when you have a name like The Main Event, you better be able to live up to it.

Anyway, the game is going on and he's getting a few points inside, making rebounds here and there and hitting from outside. Then it started to get interesting.

His defender on the other team started talking trash to him, saying stuff like:

"The Main Event is all hype."

"The Main Event is overrated."

"The Main Event is gonna be when I shut you down!"

You know the kind of stuff that can make a guy angry or motivated. Well, he got angry *and* motivated. He didn't talk back or scream or anything like that. He just got this look in his eyes that told you something was coming.

He called for the ball on the next possession and dribbled up court kind of slow, making sure that his defender was on him. And at the same time making sure all eyes were on him.

Then he dribbles up real slow on the left-hand side of the court and calls for a clear-out. All the other players on his team move over to give him some room to operate. I had never seen this guy before, so I didn't know what to expect.

He starts dribbling kind of slow from side to side, trying to lull his defender into stealing the ball, but his man doesn't fall for it. So then he goes a little faster. First to the right, then to the left. He hesitates just enough that he fakes his man right out of his shoes and takes off to his left, headed for the basket. That move alone gets the crowd going! But he's not done. As he heads for the basket, two players from the other team come over to help out on defense, but looking at his eyes, you know something good is coming.

GET THIS. WHEN HE LANDED, HE LOOKED AT THE GUY DEFENDING HIM—
YOU KNOW, THE ONE WHO WAS TALKING STUFF TO HIM EARLIER—

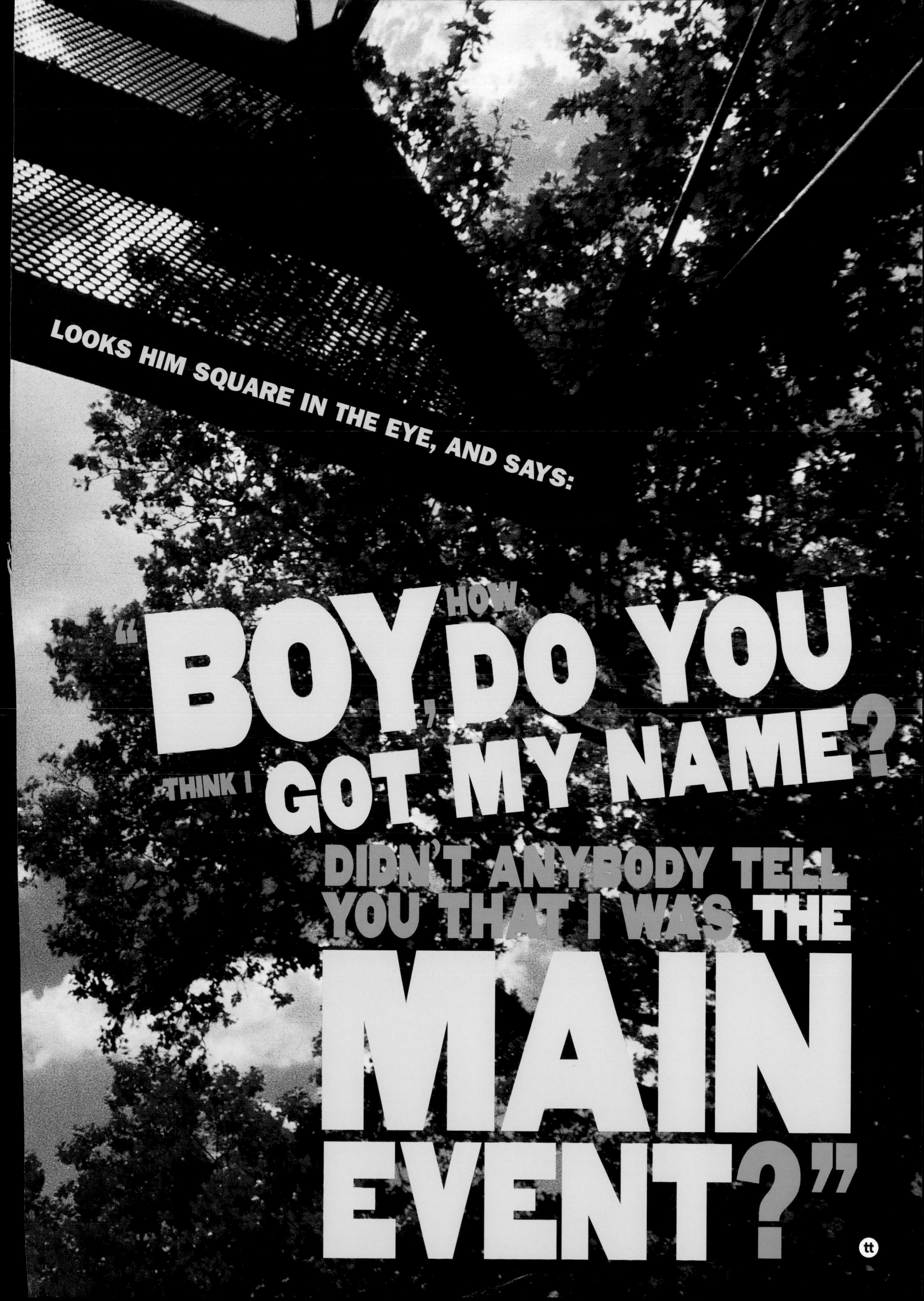
LOOKS HIM SQUARE IN THE EYE, AND SAYS:
“BOY, HOW DO YOU
THINK I GOT MY NAME?
DIDN’T ANYBODY TELL
YOU THAT I WAS THE
MAIN
EVENT?”

INSPIRATIONS

My love for the game of basketball is surpassed only by my joy in writing about and photographing it. Through words and pictures, I hope to express to you the love, pain, rhythm, and triumph that I experience when I witness a great game, team, or player. During the course of doing this book, instead of reading different authors and looking at other people's pictures, I did what most lovers of basketball would do on a lazy summer afternoon: watched lots of games and took notes. Being on the street courts made me more aware of all my senses, and that helped me to put the book together. My eyes witnessed amazing ball handling, shots, and dunks. My ears heard the coarse shuffle of sneakers on concrete, the voices of the players calling for the ball in different ways, and the shouts of the crowd responding to a great move or putting some "hotshot" in his place. My nose smelled the sweat that comes from playing for hours nonstop. My hands felt the grit on the concrete and the steel of the chain-link fences, as I moved around the court for different camera angles. My mouth became dry one too many times watching a game in the hot sun until it was done, when I quenched my thirst with a cool drink. My imagination used all of my senses as fuel and said, "What if . . . ?" Inspiration from my senses and imagination provided the stories you see here. The ability to tell a good story is an art that can take people to places they've never been, meet people they've never known, and experience things they never knew existed. All of this takes time and practice, but it begins with seeing and remembering a simple story and making it better. Most stories are exaggerated or unbelievable, but if you can make your friends believe that it really happened, who's to say it didn't? tt